Rabbit Ears Books is an imprint of Rabbit Ears Productions, Inc.
Published by Simon & Schuster, Inc.
1230 Avenue of the Americas
New York, New York 10020
Copyright © 1988 Rabbit Ears Productions Inc., Rowayton, Connecticut.
All rights reserved.
First Rabbit Ears paperback and cassette package, 1995.
Manufactured in the United States of America
10 9 8 7 6 5 4 3 2 1

The Library of Congress originally cataloged the hardcover edition as follows:
The Emperor and the Nightingale / H.C. Andersen; illustrated by Robert Van Nutt;
translated by Eva Le Gallienne.
Adaptation of: NATTERGALEN.
Summary: Despite being neglected by the emperor for a jewel-studded bird, the
little nightingale revives the dying ruler with a beautiful song.
ISBN 0-88708-087-1 (book and cassette pkg.)
[1. Fairy tales. 2. Nightingales—Fiction.] I. Andersen, H.C. (Hans Christian),
1805-1875. Nattergalen. II. Van Nutt, Robert, ill. III. Title.
PZ8.T794Em      1988
398.2—dc20
[E]—dc19                                        88-11541

ISBN 0-689-80363-X (paperback and cassette pkg.)

In China, you know, the emperor is Chinese, and all his subjects are Chinese too. It is many years since the story I am going to tell you happened, but that's all the more reason for telling it. It would be a pity if it were forgotten.

The emperor had the most beautiful palace in all the world. It was made of porcelain, so delicate and fragile you had to be very careful how you moved about in it.

The garden was full of exquisite flowers: on the rarest and most beautiful, tiny silver bells were hung, so that people passing by would be sure to notice them. Indeed, everything in the emperor's garden had been most ingeniously planned, and it was so large that the gardener himself didn't know the full extent of it. If you kept on walking long enough, you came to a wonderful forest with great trees and fathomless lakes. The forest grew all the way down to the deep blue sea; the trees stretched their branches over the water, and large ships could sail right under them.

Here lived a nightingale who sang so sweetly that even the poor fisherman—who had so much else to attend to—would stop and listen to her as he drew in his nets at night.

"How beautiful that is!" he would say; then he had to get back to his work and forget about the bird. But the next night when he came to tend his nets and heard her singing, he would say again, "How beautiful that is!"

Travelers from all over the world came to the emperor's city. They were filled with admiration for it, and for the palace and the garden. But when they heard the nightingale, they all exclaimed, "That's the loveliest thing of all!"

of his city, his palace, and his garden. "But the nightingale is the loveliest thing of all," the books said.

"What's this?" cried the emperor. "The nightingale? I've never heard of her! To think that there is such a bird in my empire—in my very own garden—and no one has told me about her. I have to read about her in a book? It's positively disgraceful!"

When they returned home, the travelers told all about their visits, and the scholars wrote many books describing the city, the palace, and the garden—but not one of them forgot the nightingale; they saved their highest praise for her. And those who could, wrote exquisite poems about the nightingale who lived in the forest by the deep blue sea.

These books went all over the world, and at last some of them reached the emperor. He sat in his gold chair reading and reading, every now and then nodding his head with pleasure when he came to an especially magnificent description

So he sent for his chamberlain, who was so very haughty that if anyone of inferior rank dared to address him or ask him a question, he only deigned to answer, "Peh!"—which of course means nothing at all.

"I understand there is a highly remarkable bird here called the nightingale," said the emperor. "They say she is the loveliest thing in my whole empire. Why has no one told me about her?"

"I've never heard that name before," answered the chamberlain. "She's not been presented at court, I'm sure of that."

"I want her to come here this very evening and sing for me," declared the emperor. "It seems the whole world knows that I possess this marvel, yet I myself know nothing about her."

"No! I have never heard that name," the chamberlain repeated. "But I shall look for her, and most certainly shall find her."

But where was he to look?

He ran up and down all the staircases, through all the halls and corridors, asking everyone he met about the nightingale. But no one knew anything about her.

"Tsing-pet!" cried the chamberlain, and he started running again, up and down the staircases, through all the halls and corridors, and half the court went with him, for they didn't want to have their stomachs pounded—particularly after supper!

They inquired right and left about the marvelous nightingale, who was known all over the world but had never been heard of by the courtiers in the palace.

At last he ran back to the emperor saying, "It must be some fantastic story invented by the people who write books. Your Imperial Majesty shouldn't pay attention to everything that's written down. It's pure imagination—what we call black magic."

"But I read this in a book sent me by the high and mighty emperor of Japan—therefore it must be true! I insist on hearing the nightingale. She must be here this very evening. I am graciously inclined toward her—and if you fail to produce her you'll all get your stomachs pounded immediately after supper!"

At last they found a poor little girl working in the kitchen. She said, "Oh, the nightingale! I know her well. How beautifully she sings! Every evening I'm allowed to take some scraps of food to my poor sick mother who lives down by the shore. On my way back I feel tired and sit down to rest a moment in the forest, and then I hear the nightingale. She sounds so beautiful that tears come to my eyes; it's as though my mother were kissing me."

"Little kitchen maid," said the chamberlain, "I'll see that you're given a permanent position in the palace kitchen, and you shall be even allowed to watch the emperor eat his dinner, if only you will lead us to the nightingale."

So, the chamberlain, the little girl, and half the court set out toward the forest. After they had walked some way, the courtiers cried, "Ah! There she is! What a powerful voice for such a little creature. But we seem to have heard her before."

"That's only a cow mooing," said the little kitchen maid. "We still have a good way to go." They passed the marshes. "I hear her!" shouted the chamberlain. "Lovely! She sounds just like the brass temple gong."

"Those are the frogs croaking," said the little kitchen maid. "But we ought to hear her soon."

And so they traveled to the very edge of the sea where the nightingale lived.

"Oh!" said the little girl. "Look up there! Do you see her?" And she pointed to a little gray bird perched high up in the branches.

"Is it possible?" said the chamberlain. "I never thought she'd look like that! She's so drab and ordinary. . . . But perhaps the sight of so many distinguished people has caused her to lose color."

"Little nightingale!" the little kitchen maid called out. "Our gracious emperor would like to hear you sing."

"With pleasure!" said the nightingale, and she sang so that it was a joy to hear her.

"It's like the tinkling of crystal bells," said the chamberlain. "And look at her little throat—how it throbs! It seems odd that we've never heard her before. She'll have a great success at court."

"Shall I sing for the emperor again?" asked the nightingale, who thought the emperor must be present.

"Most excellent little nightingale!" said the chamberlain. "It is my pleasure to invite you to appear at court this evening, where you will delight His Imperial Majesty with your enchanting song."

"It sounds best out in the forest," replied the nightingale. But since it was the emperor's wish, she agreed to go.

The emperor had ordered that the palace be scrubbed and polished until the walls and the floors, which as you may remember were made of porcelain, sparkled in the light of thousands of golden lamps. The finest flowers, those with the silver bells on them, were placed in all the corridors. There was such a-coming and going, and such a draft, that all the little bells tinkled so loudly you could hardly hear yourself speak.

In the middle of the great presence chamber, where the emperor sat on his throne, the chamberlain installed a golden perch for the nightingale.

Then, the entire court was assembled.

The little kitchen maid, who had received the title of Assistant-Cook-to-His-Imperial-Majesty, was allowed to stand behind the door.

The courtiers, dressed in their grandest clothes, all leaned forward to stare at the little gray bird. The emperor nodded graciously.

And the nightingale sang.

Tears came to the emperor's eyes and trickled down his cheeks. And the nightingale sang even more beautifully. It was enough to melt your heart. The emperor was so delighted, he wanted to give the nightingale his gold slipper to wear around her neck. But the nightingale declined this great honor.

"I have seen tears in the emperor's eyes. What could be more precious to me? And emperor's tears have a mysterious power. I have been amply rewarded." And she sang again in that sweet, ravishing voice of hers.

"Oh, how delightfully charming," exclaimed the court ladies, and they filled their mouths with water and made gurgling sounds in their throats whenever anyone spoke to them. They imagined they were nightingales too! Even the lackeys and the chambermaids admitted to being quite pleased—and that's saying a lot, for they are the most difficult people in the world to satisfy. Yes! The nightingale was a great success.

From then on she had to remain at court. She had a cage of her own, and was granted permission to go out twice during the day and once at night; but she had to be accompanied by twelve servants, each holding tightly to a silk thread fastened to her leg.

The imperial city talked of nothing but the wonderful bird. When two people met on the street, one of them had only to say "nightin" for the other to say "gale"; then they would sigh in perfect understanding. "Ahh!"

Eleven shopkeepers' children were named after the nightingale—though not one of them could sing a note, and they were tone deaf into the bargain.

One day a large parcel arrived for the emperor, and on it was written, "Nightingale."

"I expect it's a new book about our famous bird," said the emperor; but it wasn't a book at all. It was a wonderful example of the jeweler's art, lying in a velvet-lined case—an artificial nightingale that was supposed to be a copy of the real one, only it was encrusted with diamonds, rubies, and sapphires. When you wound it up, it sang one of the real nightingale's songs and its tail moved up and down and glittered with silver and gold. Around its neck was a little ribbon with the inscription "The emperor of Japan's nightingale is poor compared with that of the emperor of China."

"How marvelous!" they all cried; and the messenger who had brought the artificial bird was immediately given the title of Chief-Imperial-Nightingale-Bringer.

"Now let us hear my two nightingales sing together—what a duet that will be!" So they sang together, but it didn't turn out very well at all, for the song was stilted and mechanical. "The new bird is in no way to blame," said the music master. "It keeps perfect time and obeys all the rules of my special method."

Then the artificial bird sang by itself and had just as great a success as the real one. And it was so much more beautiful to look at. It sparkled and shimmered like some fantastic jewel.

It sang its one and only tune thirty-three times without ever getting tired. The courtiers would have liked to hear it over and over again, but the emperor felt that it was the real nightingale's turn to sing a bit. But where was she? No one had noticed that in all the excitement, she had flown out of the open window, back to her green forest.

"Here's a nice state of affairs!" cried the emperor. The courtiers were all furious and accused the nightingale of rank ingratitude.

"Well! After all, we still have the better of the two birds!" So the artificial nightingale was made to sing again, and though they now heard the tune for the thirty-fourth time, they were still quite amazed. The music master said rather loudly, "The artificial bird sings more beautifully than the real one, for its outer covering of diamonds conceals the most delicate and intricate of mechanisms.

"You see, ladies and gentlemen—and, first and foremost, Your Imperial Majesty—the real nightingale is totally unpredictable. She sings on the spur of the moment, and there's no way of knowing what you're going to hear. Whereas, with the artificial bird everything has been regulated beforehand. You get just what you expect; there are no surprises. The mechanism can be logically explained. You can take the bird apart and examine the intricate wheels and cylinders, how one minute cog fits into another, causing it to sing. It's amazing what human skill and ingenuity are able to accomplish!"

"You're absolutely right," they all agreed.

And the very next Sunday the music master
was authorized to demonstrate the bird
to the common people. "They must hear it sing
too," said the emperor. And so they did hear it
and were so delighted they seemed quite
intoxicated, as though they'd drunk too much
tea—for that's what the Chinese drink,
you know.

But the poor fisherman who had heard the
real nightingale sing said, "Yes! It's pretty
enough; it's a fairly good imitation, but there's
something lacking—I can't explain just
what it is."

The chamberlain banished the real
nightingale from the empire.

The artificial bird was placed on a silk cushion by the emperor's bed. Around it were placed all the presents that had been sent to it, all made of gold and precious stones. Its title had been raised to High-Imperial-Bedside-Table-Singer, First-Class-on-the-Left. The emperor considered the side nearer his heart to be the more distinguished.

A whole year passed. By now the emperor, the court, and all the Chinese people knew every note and every trill of the artificial bird's song and they enjoyed it all the more. It was all perfectly delightful.

But one evening, when the artificial bird was singing away and the emperor lay on his bed listening to it, something went "Crack!" inside the bird. There was a great whirring of wheels, and the song stopped.

The emperor leapt out of bed and sent for his personal physician, who could do nothing. A watchmaker was summoned, and after a great deal of talk and a long and careful examination, he managed to fix the mechanism fairly well, but he said it shouldn't be used too often, as many of the cogs had worn down and would be almost impossible to replace.

He couldn't guarantee that the song would ever be the same again. It was a tragic state of affairs. The emperor allowed the artificial bird to sing only once a year, and even that put quite a strain on it. But the music master made a little speech, full of complicated words, declaring that the song was just as good as ever; and of course that settled it. Everyone agreed it was just as good as ever!

Five more years went by, when suddenly the emperor fell ill. The whole country grieved— for the people were devoted to their emperor, and the doctors said that he hadn't long to live.

A new emperor had already been chosen, and the people stood outside in the street asking the chamberlain if there was any hope of their old emperor getting well again.

"Peh!" said the chamberlain, and shook his head.

Thick felt was laid down in the halls and corridors to muffle the sound of footsteps; the palace was as quiet as a tomb.

The emperor lay in his huge, magnificent bed, so cold and so pale that the courtiers thought him already dead, and they all dashed off to pay court to the new emperor. The lackeys ran outside to gossip about it, and the chambermaids gave a large tea party.

But the emperor wasn't dead. He lay there stiff and pale in his magnificent bed with the long velvet hangings and the heavy gold tassels. High up in the wall was an open window through which the moon shone down upon him and on the artificial bird by his side.

But the poor emperor could hardly breathe. He felt something heavy weighing on his chest; he opened his eyes and saw that it was Death. Death was wearing the emperor's gold crown, and held the gold sword of state in one hand and the imperial banner in the other; and from the folds of the heavy velvet bed-hangings strange faces peered out—some hideous and evil, others mild and gentle.

These were the emperor's good and bad deeds watching him as he lay there with Death weighing on his heart. "Do you remember this?" they whispered to him, one after another. "Do

you remember that?" And they reminded him of many, many things—and the sweat stood out on his brow.

"I never knew about all that!" cried the emperor. "Music! Music! Strike up the great gong and drown out their voices!"

But the voices continued, Death nodding his head in agreement with all that was said.

"Music! Music!" the emperor cried again. "Precious little golden bird, sing to me! Sing! I implore you, sing! I've showered you with gold and precious jewels. I even hung my gold slipper around your neck with my own hands. Sing to me now! Sing!"

But the bird was silent. And the silence grew more and more terrifying. Death stared down at the emperor with great, hollow eyes.

Suddenly, through the window, came the sound of an exquisite song. It was the living nightingale, perched on a branch outside. She had heard of the emperor's suffering and came to bring him hope. She sang, and the blood began to flow more swiftly through the emperor's feeble body. Death himself listened, saying, "Sing, little nightingale! Sing on!"

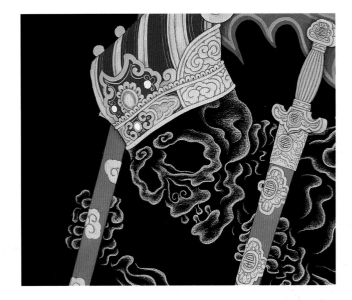

"Yes! If you will give up the golden sword! If you will give up the imperial banner! If you will give up the emperor's golden crown!"

She sang of the peaceful graveyard where the white roses bloom, where the air is sweet with the scent of the elder tree, where the green grass is moistened by the tears of those who grieve. And, as he listened, Death was filled with a great longing to be back in his own garden, and he vanished out of the window like a cold white mist.

The nightingale sang, and the emperor fell into a gentle, refreshing sleep.

The next morning he awoke to find himself well and strong again. His servants were gone, for they thought he was dead, but the nightingale was still singing.

"You must never leave me!" cried the emperor. "You need only sing when you feel like singing, and I shall smash the artificial bird into a thousand pieces."

"Don't do that!" said the nightingale. "It did the best it could. Keep it with you. I can't settle down and live here in the palace. Let me come and go as I like. I'll sit on the branch outside your window and sing to you, so that your thoughts may be serene and joyful."

And so the nightingale sang freely for fisherman, farmer, kitchen maid, and emperor alike. And the emperor ruled wisely and well for a long, long time.